Ollie's Tonsils

Hospital Adventures

By Tony Densley and Niki Palmer

Hospital Adventures

Ollie's Tonsils
Copyright © 2016 by Beanz books
Authors Tony Densley and Niki Palmer
Illustrated by Michelle Berlin

Third Edition 2019

ISBN 9781925422184

Once again, Ollie woke up with a sore throat. Ouch.

The next day Mummy took Ollie to see Doctor Lewis, who asked Ollie to open his mouth, stick his tongue out and say "Aaaaaah.

Dr Lewis gently examined Ollie by putting a wooden stick like an icy pole stick in his mouth to hold his wiggly tongue still. He had a light like a torch on his head so he could see into Ollie's red sore throat.

Ollie's throat had been sore many times before, so Doctor Lewis said: "We need to help you with your tonsils, Ollie."

"What are tonsils?" Ollie asked.

"Tonsils are the two little things on either side of the little dangly bit in the back of your throat. Their job is to help stop yucky germs getting into your body," replied Doctor Lewis.

"But sometimes they get so big from working hard killing germs that they hurt when you swallow, and so we take care of them, to make your throat feel better."

"I think you need a trip to the hospital for an operation then you won't have such bad sore throats."

"Will it hurt?" asked Ollie. "I have not had an operation before."

Doctor Lewis explained, "The operation won't hurt, but your throat will be a bit sore and scratchy for a week or so afterwards. It's a bit like when you fall over and scrape your knee; it takes a while for it to heal."

Ollie didn't like the sound of that; he didn't want to go to the hospital as he was scared. He didn't want his tonsils to be gone.   He needed   those!

"You don't need your tonsils, Ollie," added Doctor Lewis. "There are many other ways to block yucky germs. This operation will stop your sore throats."

Mummy said "It will be okay; a hospital is a nice place. Full of friendly doctors and nurses who will look after you and I will be there all the time too."

After dinner, Ollie helped Mum pack his bag to take to the hospital in case he needed to stay overnight.

She put in a book, a toothbrush and toothpaste, pyjamas and an extra set of clothes.

After an operation, some children can go home the same day, but others need to stay overnight until they are well enough to go home.

Ollie made sure Mum packed his favourite Teddy Bear for him to cuddle on his first time sleeping away from home.

Ollie and Mum laughed as this was going to be Teddy's first time away as well so they could cuddle each other!

The next morning Mum woke Ollie up early. "Come on, Ollie; it's time to go to the hospital," Mum called.

"But I haven't had my breakfast yet," said Ollie.

"Sorry Ollie, Doctor Lewis told me you could not have anything to eat before the operation, only a couple of sips of water."

"After the operation, you will have ice cream and some other cool treats to eat."

"Ok, let me just say goodbye to Alfie, he is going to wonder where I am." Ollie patted his little dog and gave him a big hug.

When they arrived at the hospital, Mummy went to the front desk so the doctor would know Ollie was ready for his operation.

The lady behind the desk said, "Hello Ollie. Are you coming to stay with us tonight?"

"We have a bed picked out for you just down the hall."

At the hospital, everybody had a uniform on, but in different colours, blue, green, and purple. Ollie thought it was quite funny as some looked like they were wearing pyjamas. He also wondered if they slept over too, just like he would.

There was a fresh, clean smell in the hospital: like oranges, lemons and limes, it was like the smell when Mummy cleaned the bathroom to keep it safe from yucky germs.

Mummy took Ollie into a waiting room with lots of other children and parents. Some of them were also having their tonsils out that morning too just like Ollie; all the children were very hungry.

Luckily the waiting room had lots of fun toys to play with as Ollie and Mummy had to wait a long time.

A friendly nurse asked Mummy and Ollie to go into a room called the examination room, where she checked Ollie's temperature and asked Mummy lots of questions.

"What is your favourite smell?" She asked Ollie. "Strawberry or Cherry?"

"Strawberry is nice" Ollie replied.

"Ok, we will put the Strawberry smell in your superhero mask when you have your operation, so it smells great."

The nurse gave Ollie a green gown to wear. She also gave him a white plastic bracelet with his name on it. "Now everybody who works here will know your name, Ollie."

Ollie liked this idea; no-one would forget who he was.

Mummy took Ollie into a room with lots of shiny things and interesting looking machines. There was a funny big bed to lie in which went up and down and had wheels. Ollie wanted to press the buttons to see what they could do.

A man in a white coat came into the room to see Ollie. It was Doctor Lewis. He took Ollie's blood pressure and listened to Ollie's heart with a special gadget called a stethoscope.

Doctor Lewis let Ollie listen to his own heart with the stethoscope as well. It beat like this: Thumpa, thumpa, thump... Thumpa, thumpa, thump!

A short time later, a friendly man in a red shirt came into the room.

"Hi Ollie, my name is John, my job is to take you to the operating theatre where Doctor Lewis is waiting."

He wheeled Ollie's bed through the hallways. This way and that. John knew exactly where to go. Ollie's Mummy walked beside him. Ollie thought it was like being on a roller coaster, right there in the hospital.

Soon they went into a white room where a lady wearing a bright purple uniform was waiting.

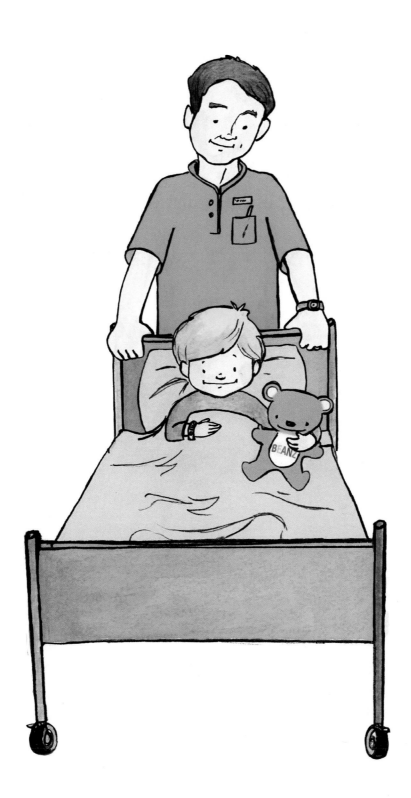

"Hi!" I'm Doctor Rachael, and I'm an anaesthetist. My job is to give you special medicine, so you'll fall asleep before your operation. That way you won't see, hear or feel a thing! You'll go to sleep and when you wake up your sore tonsils will be gone."

"I will stay with you the whole time and make sure you are ok."

Ollie lay back on his bed. "See this mask?" said Rachael. "You're going to be just like Super Ollie, the superhero! Put it on, and you'll fly to sleep, and before you know it, your operation will be all over!"

Then Doctor Rachael put a mask on Ollie's face, and after a few deep breaths of the yummy strawberry smell, Ollie went right to sleep. And that's when Doctor Lewis took out Ollie's tonsils.

The next thing he knew, Ollie was lying in a different room, called the recovery room and his operation was over. He was still sleepy and had a hard time keeping his eyes open. "Don't worry Ollie. You're okay now. You're still a little sleepy, but you'll wake up soon." Mum said.

A little while later, when Ollie woke up properly, John the friendly porter was there to take him and Mum to his room where other children were sleeping after their operations.

Ollie had a little tube, thinner than a straw, in his arm. It was called an IV, and it was there to give him special medicine and liquids. With his sore throat, he didn't feel like drinking, so he was glad it was there.

He also had a tube just under his nose to give him more oxygen to help him breathe. He didn't really like this tube but knew he had to have it for a little while to help him get better.

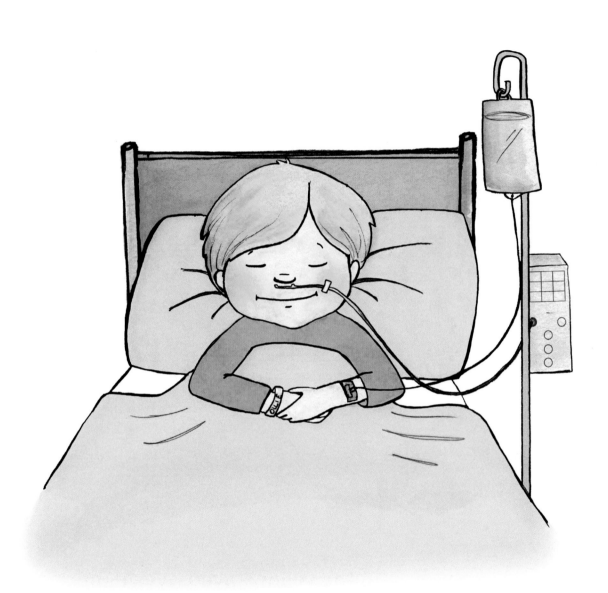

Ollie stayed overnight in the hospital so the nurses could make sure that his throat was ok.

And mum was right. Soon Ollie felt a bit better, his throat was still a little scratchy and sore but not like all those other times when his throat hurt. He sat in bed sipping a cold drink the nurse had given him and occasionally going back to sleep.

He had his favourite pyjamas to wear and his best-loved teddy bear to snuggle with in bed. Daddy came to visit him, and Ollie showed him the magic buttons that made the bed move.

All the other children in the room stayed overnight as well. It was like having a sleepover at a friend's house, but with more bloops and bleeps from the neat machines.

A lovely, friendly nurse was there, to watch over him and keep him safe, and Mummy stayed all night with him, too.

The next morning, Doctor Lewis visited Ollie to check his throat. He looked in his mouth and felt his neck, and then listened to his heart one more time. It went Thumpa, thumpa, thump just like before.

Doctor Lewis told him, "You look a lot better Ollie; you can go home today but remember to drink lots of cool drinks and take your medicine to help your throat get better quickly."

"Hooray!" said Ollie. "I can go home and see Alfie, my dog I've missed him."

To make it easy to get dressed Mummy had packed Ollie's favourite button up shirt, so she did not have to pull anything over his head and hurt his neck or throat.

Ollie said "thank you" to the Nurse for looking after him. All the staff waved goodbye to Ollie and said they hoped he enjoyed his short stay in the hospital.

Then Mummy drove him home; she even had a plastic bucket in the car in case Ollie wanted to be sick as he was a little upset in his tummy!

When Ollie got home, he still had a bit of a sore throat for a few days. Ollie's Mummy remembered he had to drink lots of cold drinks and take his medicine to help his sore throat get better, so she made him fruit smoothies and gave him some water and juice.

She also made lots of easy to eat food like applesauce and cookies and soup and sandwiches. Ollie loved to eat anything that made his throat feel better. But Ice cream was his favourite!

While Ollie was getting better, he had to remember to wash his hands many times a day, so he did not catch any yucky germs, especially after playing with Alfie or being outside. "Keeping hands clean helps children stay healthy and strong," Mummy told him.

It had taken a whole week before Ollie felt like he wanted to run around with Alfie in the garden and play like usual.

Ollie was happy he did not have any more sore throats as he did before and was glad, he had been brave and had his tonsils operation. At the time he was scared, but it was OK, and he was so happy that he did it because now he felt so much better all the time.

He was glad he could eat his favourite peanut butter on toast without it hurting his throat, and that life was now back to normal.

Remember, it's okay to feel scared if you must go to the hospital for an operation. But with the help of an adult and the kind nurses, doctors, porters, and other people who work there, you will have a safe stay at the hospital.

You will see new things (like big machines). You will smell new things, too, and you will make new friends.

It will be a great adventure!

The End

beanz books

Alice's Wonderful Hospital Adventure

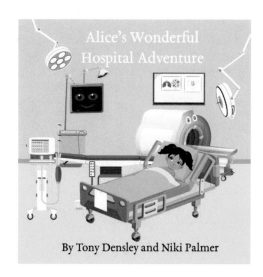

Smelly Melly
Personal Hygiene for Kids & Little Monsters

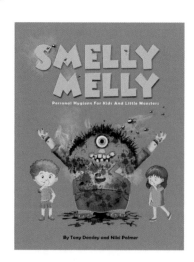

Made in the USA
Monee, IL
16 September 2022